Butterfly Wishes

Spring Shine Sparkles

D0981557

The Butterfly Wishes series

The Wishing Wings

Tiger Streak's Tale

Blue Rain's Adventure

Spring Shine Sparkles

Butterfly Wishes

Spring Shine Sparkles

WITHDRAWN

Jennifer Castle

illustrated by Tracy Bishop

BLOOMSBURY

NEW YORK LONDON OXFORD NEW DELHI SYDNEY

First published in the United States of America in April 2018
by Bloomsbury Children's Books
www.bloomsbury.com

Bloomsbury is a registered trademark of Bloomsbury Publishing Plc

For information about permission to reproduce selections from this book, write to
Permissions, Bloomsbury Children's Books, 1385 Broadway, New York, New York 10018
Bloomsbury books may be purchased for business or promotional use. For information on
bulk purchases please contact Macmillan Corporate and Premium Sales Department at
specialmarkets@macmillan.com

Library of Congress Cataloging-in-Publication Data
Names: Castle, Jennifer, author.
Title: Spring Shine sparkles / by Jennifer Castle.
Description: New York : Bloomsbury, 2018. | Series: Butterfly wishes ; 4 |
Summary: Sisters Addie and Clara bring together a newly emerged Wishing
Wings butterfly, Spring Shine, and Addie's best friend, Violet, both of
whom are feeling bad about themselves.
Identifiers: LCCN 2017021643 (print) | LCCN 2017037382 (e-book)
ISBN 978-1-68119-377-9 (paperback) • ISBN 978-1-68119-692-3 (hardcover)
ISBN 978-1-68119-378-6 (e-book)
Subjects: | CYAC: Butterflies—Fiction. | Self-esteem—Fiction. |
Friendship—Fiction. | Wishes—Fiction. | Magic—Fiction. | Sisters—Fiction.
Classification: LCC PZ7.C268732 Spr 2018 (print) | LCC PZ7.C268732 (e-book)
DDC [Fic]—dc23
LC record available at https://lccn.loc.gov/2017021643

Typeset by Westchester Publishing Services
Printed and bound in the U.S.A. by Berryville Graphics Inc., Berryville, Virginia
2 4 6 8 10 9 7 5 3 1 (paperback)
2 4 6 8 10 9 7 5 3 1 (hardcover)

All papers used by Bloomsbury Publishing, Inc., are natural, recyclable products
made from wood grown in well-managed forests. The manufacturing processes
conform to the environmental regulations of the country of origin.

For Jamie Weiss Chilton,
who sparkles and shines

Butterfly Wishes

Spring Shine Sparkles

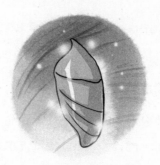

PROLOGUE

All through Wishing Wing Grove, everything was still as stone.

The wildflowers didn't move. The leaves on the trees didn't rustle. There were no morning breezes in the air. Even the four colorful butterflies gathered on the trunk of a giant willow tree didn't flutter a single wing. The entire grove was waiting . . .

"Any minute now," said one of the butterflies.

"Any *second*, really," said another.

"The anticipation is driving me crazy!" a third said.

"She'll come out soon enough," said the fourth butterfly, whose name was Sky Dance.

These were Wishing Wing butterflies, covered in brilliant colors and patterns, possessing the power to do extraordinary magic.

The four Wishing Wings crept closer to the edge of a hollow in the tree's trunk

and peered at a single gray chrysalis hanging inside. Next to the chrysalis were the scrunched-up remains of three other chrysalides that had already popped open.

"This dark enchantment is so sneaky," said Sky Dance to the others. "It kept the three of you from knowing you had to earn your magic by granting a wish to a human child before sunset. Someone wanted you to lose your magic, because it would make all Wishing Wing magic get weaker and possibly disappear. The enchantment worked in different ways

on each of you, and we have no idea what it will do to our friend."

"Whatever happens," one of the butterflies said, puffing up her furry chest, "we'll be ready to help."

"That's right!" said another, stretching her wings as tall and straight as she could. "We'll do whatever it takes!"

"We'll find out who cursed us, too!" added the third, curling her antennae into angry horns. "Nobody tries to destroy or steal Wishing Wing magic and gets away with it!"

Sky Dance smiled. "We'll need all that courage, for sure. Especially if we have to travel to the far side of the meadow."

All four butterflies nodded at one another, serious and determined . . . but also a bit nervous.

Then, the entire grove went back to

being still and silent, as if even the flowers, trees, and air knew that this last
chrysalis was about to open.

Or was it?

CHAPTER ONE

A brown cardboard box sat in the corner of Addie Gibson's bedroom, looking lonely and forgotten. The words *DESK STUFF* were written in red marker across the top.

Addie had been staring at this box all morning. It was the last one she needed to unpack since her family had moved from the city to a house in the country.

But she was having trouble doing it. The box was filled with things she'd need for her new school, which would be starting in a couple of weeks. Thinking about her new school gave Addie an instant, nervous lump in her throat. Opening the box meant it would all be way too real, way too soon.

"Okay," she said to the box. "Enough is enough. Let's do this."

The box seemed okay with that.

Addie dragged it into the middle of the room, sat down on the floor, tore open the packing tape, and reached her hand inside.

First, she found a stationery set decorated with her initials. Next, a case of colored pens and some erasers shaped like cupcakes. Then, a notebook with an adorable baby bunny on the cover, and an old cookie tin filled with tape, scissors, and glue. Finally, Addie's fingers found the sharp corners of what might be a book. When she pulled it out, she gasped in surprise.

Her old diary!

It was the fancy kind, a hardcover with thick, blank pages that smelled a little like flowers and a little like a library. Addie flipped through it, recognizing her own neat handwriting in blue pen. She used to write in the diary every night, right before bed. She'd loved recording the events of each day and the feelings that went along with them. But halfway through the book, the handwriting ended; all the pages after that were empty.

Addie knew exactly when she'd stopped writing in the diary. It was the night her parents told her they would be

moving to a place called Brook Forest, hours away from everything she'd ever known and especially from her best friend, Violet. Addie had been so upset, she'd cried on and off for days. Why would she want to remember that kind of sadness?

But those feelings were fading fast. Her first week in Brook Forest had been filled with the most amazing and wonderful happenings. Those events belonged in her diary! Addie grabbed a pen from the case, turned to the first blank page, and began to write.

Dear Diary, Guess what? In the woods behind our new house, there's a place called Wishing Wing Grove. It's the home of the Wishing Wing butterflies, who can make magic by turning one thing into another. My butterfly BFF is named Sky Dance. She's basically a princess because her mother is the queen, Rose Glow. Clara also has a butterfly BFF: Sky Dance's sister Shimmer Leaf. They came to us for help because there's a dark enchantment on a group of New Blooms, which are Wishing Wings that have just changed from caterpillars to butterflies. So far we've broken the enchantment on three butterflies and helped them earn their magic: Shimmer Leaf, Tiger Streak, and Blue Rain. There's one more left, but we still haven't figured out who cast the enchantment and caused all this trouble in the first place.

Addie stopped and read what she wrote. Did it sound crazy? Well, yes. Of course. But so what? This was for her eyes only. It felt great to begin telling the story of her new life.

Addie shifted the diary in her lap, and a photo fell out from between two pages. When she picked it up, she recognized it instantly: a snapshot of herself and Violet at a school Halloween party. Violet was dressed as a half-angel, half-devil; Addie was Dorothy from *The Wizard of Oz*. The memory of that party, and all the other fun times with Violet, flooded her with a happy-sad feeling. She had already made new friends in Brook Forest, but Violet would always be special. Addie ran her fingers over the gold bracelet on her wrist. When she'd first met Sky Dance and made a wish to stay close to Violet forever, the butterfly had made the bracelet for her. The bracelet was filled with magic that would keep the girls' friendship strong.

"Are you missing Violet?" asked a high, musical voice.

Addie looked up to see a very familiar pair of butterfly wings on her window sill. They were pink and turquoise, with cloud patterns on them.

"Sky Dance!" Addie exclaimed. "Please come in!"

Sky Dance fluttered into the room and flew a slow loop around it before landing on Addie's bedpost. "So this is your hollow," she said with an approving nod of her furry pink head. "I like it!"

"Thanks," Addie said. "It's no Wishing Wing Grove, but it's cozy. Are you here because the last New Bloom has come out?"

"Actually," Sky Dance began with a sigh, "I'm here because she *hasn't* come out. We've all been waiting and waiting! Everyone's afraid that Spring Shine— that's her name —won't emerge at all. It's really stressful. I decided to visit you instead."

"That does sound nerve-racking," agreed Addie. "I'm glad you came."

"I'm worried, Addie. Even if we can break Spring Shine's enchantment like we did for Shimmer Leaf, Tiger Streak, and Blue Rain, we still don't know who cast it in the first place. The next set of New Blooms could be in danger the same way."

"I know," Addie said. "I was thinking about that, too. Let's focus on making sure Spring Shine's okay. Then we can try to solve this mystery."

There was a sudden, loud *rap rap rap* on Addie's door. Addie's heart leaped; if it was her mother, she'd have to hide Sky Dance. Maybe the butterfly could pretend to be one of the glass animal figurines on Addie's bookshelf.

"Addie, who are you talking to?" asked Clara's voice.

Phew, thought Addie. "Come in and you'll see," she replied.

Clara burst in, holding her new kitten, Squish (who used to be a stuffed toy kitten, before Wishing Wing magic made him real). When Clara spotted Sky Dance, she smiled. "Oh, good. You're both here! Shimmer Leaf just sent me a thought message that Spring Shine's chrysalis is starting to open!"

Because Shimmer Leaf was Clara's Wishing Wing, they could send messages to each other with their thoughts. Addie and Sky Dance could do the same.

Sky Dance sailed excitedly into the air and flew a figure eight. "Let's go! I'll meet you outside!"

Clara put down Squish and grabbed her purple satin backpack from her room. Then both girls thundered downstairs to put on their sneakers. Their mother was in the kitchen, typing out a message on her phone. When she saw Addie and Clara, she quickly tucked the phone away.

"Where are you two headed in such a rush?" asked Mom.

"One of our magic butterfly friends needs us in the woods!" said Clara.

Addie felt panic rush through her. Why would Clara spill their secret just like that?

But then her mother laughed.

"You girls are so creative with your games. By all means, go outside and play! I need you back here by noon, though. There's a surprise coming, and you don't want to miss it."

The girls nodded on their way out the back door. Sky Dance had flown out the window and was waiting for them on the deck railing. Once they were crossing the line of evenly spaced trees that separated their backyard from the woods, Addie turned to Clara. "Why did you tell Mom about the butterflies?"

"I knew she'd think it was part of a game," Clara replied. "This way, we're telling the truth about where we're going."

"Good plan," said Sky Dance. "Come on, we have to hurry if we want to see Spring Shine emerge!"

Addie had never seen a butterfly come out of its chrysalis, let alone a *magic* and probably *cursed* butterfly, so she broke into a run. Clara followed, with Sky Dance fluttering at top speed above their heads. The first few days in Brook Forest, these woods had freaked Addie out. Now, she and Clara knew the way to Wishing Wing Grove by heart. Soon they were dashing through the tall, waving grass of Silk Meadow, which was the entrance to the grove. Then they arrived in the realm of the Wishing Wing butterflies, a place filled with thick trees that were lush with leaves, neon-bright moss, a zillion kinds of colorful flowers (okay, maybe not that many, but it was definitely a lot), and a winding, bubbling creek.

Finally, huffing and puffing, the girls came to a stop at their destination: the Changing Tree, a gigantic willow with countless curving branches. This was the special place where caterpillars became Wishing Wing butterflies. Perched on the tree trunk, at the edge of a deep hollow in the trunk, was a butterfly with purple, peach, and mint-green wings. The leaf patterns on them made her instantly recognizable.

"Shimmer Leaf!" Clara greeted her.

On a branch right above, Addie spotted the two other New Blooms whose magic they'd already helped save: Tiger Streak (with her yellow, orange, and black tiger-striped wings) and Blue Rain (her wings deep purple and blue, with teardrop patterns).

Addie stepped up to the hollow and peered in. She saw three empty chrysalides, and one that was still full. It looked like a dull, gray pebble, except it was wiggling. Something was about to happen, for sure.

"Whoa," said Clara, stepping up beside

her. Sky Dance landed next to Shimmer Leaf. They all watched as the wiggling got faster and faster. Addie's heart sped up and she couldn't tell if it was from nervousness or excitement. A new word for it popped into her head: *Nervous-ited!*

Suddenly, the chrysalis tore open. Addie saw legs, antennae, and a furry yellow head. Then colors. Butterfly wings!

Once the little creature was completely out of the chrysalis, she planted all six legs on the wall of the hollow and slowly stretched her wings out straight.

Then Addie gasped.

CHAPTER TWO

How beautiful!

Red, orange, yellow, green, blue, indigo, and violet. All the colors of the rainbow, in stripes that swirled across Spring Shine's wings.

The brand-new butterfly blinked and looked around, her yellow eyes wide.

Addie held her breath. Would Spring

Shine know she was a Wishing Wing? When Shimmer Leaf had emerged, the dark enchantment had caused her to forget who she was. It had made Tiger Streak think she was a bee. If Spring Shine *did* know who she was, would she still be herself? The enchantment had turned Blue Rain into a cranky, nasty New Bloom who loved to insult everyone. Fortunately, the real Blue Rain was sweet and kind . . . but that had been a *very* unpleasant afternoon.

Spring Shine spotted the other four Wishing Wings, and her eyes grew even wider.

Then she smiled.

"Hello, my friends!" she said in a cheerful voice. She rocketed out of the hollow, and her friends flew in a circle around her, squealing "Welcome!," "You're here!," and "Hooray!"

Addie and Clara watched this happy reunion, and Addie felt a flood of relief. Could it be that the dark enchantment hadn't worked on Spring Shine? Maybe they wouldn't have to fight it anymore.

Spring Shine landed on the tree trunk near the girls, peering at them with curiosity.

Sky Dance landed next to her and said, "Spring Shine, I want you to meet our friends Addie and Clara."

"Humans in Wishing Wing Grove?" chirped Spring Shine. "Wow, I've missed a lot!"

"When the three of us came out," Shimmer Leaf explained, pointing one leg at Tiger Streak and one at Blue Rain, "we were under a dark enchantment designed to keep us from earning our magic. Addie and Clara helped break that enchantment. They're basically the coolest kids ever."

Addie and Clara smiled at each other. Addie thought, *If a magic butterfly thinks I'm cool, maybe it can be true.*

"How do you feel?" Sky Dance asked Spring Shine. "Anything odd? Do all your butterfly parts work?"

Spring Shine fluttered her wings, stretched all six legs, and waved her antennae around in circles. "Everything seems to be in order," she said. "How do my wings look?"

"They're gorgeous!" Addie told her.

"*Super* gorgeous," Clara agreed.

"Really? You're not just saying that, are you? Because when I was a caterpillar, I was the plainest one in the nursery.

Everyone else was a pretty color, but I was just white."

"Come to the Mirror Pool," suggested Sky Dance. "We'll show you."

Sky Dance led the other four butterflies, and Addie and Clara, to a spot behind the Changing Tree. It was a tiny pond ringed with knobby brown vines, the water smooth and clear as glass. Addie peered in and saw her own reflection, then saw Sky Dance land on her shoulder. One vine hung over the pool, stretched between two trees. Spring Shine flitted over to it. She spread her wings wide, took a deep breath, and looked down.

Then she gasped. It was the sound of shock and panic.

"No!" cried Spring Shine, and burst into tears. "Why?" she wailed. "Why?"

Addie and Clara exchanged very

confused looks. Sky Dance flew over to the vine and perched next to Spring Shine.

"What's the matter?" asked Sky Dance. "You don't like your rainbows? I think these wings are absolutely beautiful!"

"Me too!" said Shimmer Leaf. Tiger Streak and Blue Rain added their agreement as well.

"*Rainbows?*" asked Spring Shine. "What rainbows?"

"The ones right there!" Sky Dance pointed two of her legs at Spring Shine's wings.

Spring Shine looked at her reflection again. Addie could see the butterfly's colors and patterns mirrored in the water.

"I don't know what you're talking about," said Spring Shine in a shaky, broken voice. "My wings don't have any

colors or rainbows. They're white!" She spread her wings out straight and looked from one to the other. "Plain white! Oh my goodness, that must be the dark enchantment you were talking about! I've lost my magic already!"

New Blooms who couldn't earn their magic by sunset on their first day turned into plain white butterflies. Whenever Addie saw one of these, she wondered if it was a former Wishing Wing.

Sky Dance flew a circle around Spring Shine, then landed next to her again. "I think you might be right about the dark enchantment. It's keeping you from seeing your colors!"

"Stop saying I have colors," said Spring Shine with a sniffle. "I know you're just trying to make me feel better, but it's no use. Clearly, the enchantment took away my wing patterns *and* my magic."

"You must believe us!" said Clara.

This is terrible, thought Addie. *There has to be some way to show Spring Shine what she really looks like.*

She glanced at her sister, then at her sister's purple satin backpack. Clara loved to collect key chains and hang them from the zippers. There were over a dozen of them now, including a rubber penguin (adorable), a squishy car (weird), and a plastic foot (gross). Addie never understood why Clara wanted all that extra stuff on her backpack. Then she spotted one keychain in particular:

A tiny toy camera.

It wasn't really a camera. If you peered through the view finder, you'd see a 3D picture of the beach their family had visited last summer. Good thing they were hanging out with butterflies who could magically turn one thing into another.

Addie grabbed Clara's arm and whispered her idea.

"Know what? You're smart," said Clara, taking off her backpack. She slid the camera keychain off one of the zippers and held it up to Shimmer Leaf. "Oh, Shimmer! Do you think this will help Spring Shine see what her wings really look like?"

Shimmer tilted her head as she regarded the keychain, then her eyes lit up. "I get it! Yup, it sure will!"

Clara placed the keychain on a rock and stepped back. Shimmer Leaf zoomed into the air, then flew in a circle around the little camera. She left a trail of sparkling purple, peach, and mint-green stripes behind her. Another circle, and then a third. The stripes hung in the air for a few moments, sparkling like glitter. When everything faded, the keychain was gone. In its place was a real, shiny silver digital camera.

"Yay!" said Clara, clapping her hands. "Thank you, Shimmer!"

Shimmer Leaf landed on Clara's shoulder and dipped her head in a humble butterfly curtsy.

Clara gave the camera to Addie. "You're better at taking pictures than I am," she said.

Addie turned the

camera on and held it up. "Okay, Spring Shine. We're going to take a photo of you. That way, you'll have proof of what your wings really look like. Can you open them as wide as you can?"

Spring Shine wiped her tears with two of her left legs, then nodded. She spread her wings out straight. A light breeze ruffled them a bit, reminding Addie of a colorful sailboat.

She raised the camera and took a few pictures, zooming in to make sure it was an up-close shot. Addie checked the screen. There was Spring Shine in all her rainbow glory. Addie thought, *Nice! I do take good photos!*

"Come take a look!" said Sky Dance to Spring Shine. Spring Shine flew over and landed on Addie's shoulder. Addie pointed to the image on the screen.

"See!" she said.

Spring Shine stared at the picture for several very long moments.

Then she started crying again. "You guys are so mean!"

"Mean?" echoed Addie. She couldn't contain her shock. Nobody had ever called her "mean" before. Well, Clara had, but sisters don't count.

"What are you talking about?" Sky Dance asked. She sounded just as shocked as Addie.

"All I see is white wings!" exclaimed Spring Shine. "My plain, boring, unmagical white wings!"

She flew over to a nearby moss patch and started sobbing again.

Sky Dance sighed in Addie's ear. "This is the dark enchantment, for sure, making

Spring Shine think she's already lost her magic!"

Clara touched Addie's arm, then tapped her watch. "Hey, it's getting close to noon. Remember what Mom said?"

"Oh, right!" said Addie. She turned to Spring Shine, resisting the urge to reach out and stroke the butterfly. Addie hated seeing any creature so sad. "Spring Shine, would you come back to Brook Forest with us? We can help you find a kid who needs a wish."

"Save yourself the trouble!" said Spring Shine in between sobs. "It's too late for me to earn my magic."

Addie turned to Sky Dance and Shimmer Leaf. "We have to go home right now or we'll get in trouble with our mom. Will you talk to Spring Shine and convince her to come to Brook Forest? Maybe she'll listen to you."

"We'll do our best," said Shimmer Leaf, but she didn't sound at all confident.

"Send us thought messages when you have some news," added Clara.

They waved goodbye to their butterfly friends and rushed off toward home. A surprise waited for them on the other side of the woods.

CHAPTER THREE

I bet it's a trampoline!" shouted Clara as they ran through the woods. The girls knew the way home by heart at this point. There were familiar trees and bushes to use as landmarks, not to mention some funny-shaped rocks. Addie's favorite was the one that looked like a baby elephant snuggling with its mother.

"A trampoline? After cousin Alexis broke her arm on one?" Addie replied. "Uh, I don't think so."

"So what do you think the surprise is?"

Addie opened her mouth to say she was absolutely positive the surprise was a swingset. But just as they were about to pass between two thin birch trees, something stopped her:

A giant spiderweb.

It stretched from one of the trees to the other, right at eye level. Another step, and Addie would have walked right into it. She held out her arm to stop Clara.

"Watch the web!" she warned her sister.

"Weird," said Clara. "That wasn't here a little while ago. Spiders work fast, I guess."

The girls ducked under the web. A few

steps later, Addie looked up to see a familiar oak tree . . . and another spiderweb spun between the trunk of the tree and a big rock on the ground nearby. There was no way to crawl under or over it.

"Okay," said Clara as she and Addie stepped around the rock. "That's weird *and* annoying."

The girls paused. They'd gotten a bit turned around, and Addie wasn't sure which direction their next landmark might be.

"It's this way," said Clara, pointing.

"Are you sure?" Addie asked.

"Yes! Hurry, we're going to be late!"

They found three more brand-new webs before they reached their own backyard, each one slowing them down or tripping up their sense of direction. Once they'd stepped onto the back deck, they took a half-second to brush the dirt and leaves off their clothes, then walked into the kitchen.

Mom was still on her computer. She glanced up at the girls, then at her wristwatch.

"Eleven fifty-nine," she said. "Talk about cutting it close. But thank you for listening and being back when I asked."

"So what's the surprise?" asked Clara eagerly.

"I can't tell you yet," Mom teased with a smile. "You'll just have to wait and see."

"Is it a package that's being delivered?" asked Addie. "Maybe a huge package?"

Mom grinned wider, her eyes twinkling. "In a sense, yes."

Clara looked at Addie and mouthed the word *TRAMPOLINE!* Mom laughed. She was enjoying this a little too much.

"Thanks a lot, Mom," said Clara. "We rushed home and now we have to wait around?"

Suddenly, the doorbell rang.

"Addie, I'd like you to go answer that," said Mom. Now she was biting her lip, trying to hide her smile, but not really succeeding.

Addie walked down the hallway to the front door, her mother and Clara in tow. Why was *she* being asked to open it? Mom knew she felt shy about that kind of thing.

She took a deep breath, turned the knob, and flung the door open.

Then Addie gasped.

For a moment, she saw fireworks in her eyes, like when the Wishing Wings turned her into a butterfly. But no magic was happening here. At least, she didn't think so.

"Hi, you!" said the girl on their porch.

It was Violet!

Addie squealed. The next thing she knew, she and Violet were hugging and jumping up and down at the same time. They stopped for a second to bring Clara into the jumping-hug.

When they finally calmed down and stepped apart, Addie saw Violet's parents standing nearby on the porch steps.

It hadn't been that long since Addie and Violet had seen each other, but it felt like years. Addie's life was already so different. Plus, Violet looked different. Her dark-brown hair was much shorter, and now that they'd stopped laughing and screaming, there was something a little sad and quiet about her expression.

"I can't believe this!" said Clara. "What are you doing here?"

"We were on a camping trip up north," replied Violet, "and my parents arranged a little detour on our way home so we could see you."

Addie turned to Violet's parents and said, "Thank you!" Then she gave her mom a hug. "Best surprise ever, Mom."

"I had a feeling it might be," she said. "Come inside, everyone. Let's give you the grand tour!"

After they had shown Violet and her parents the entire house, and everyone had marveled over Squish's cuteness, Addie and Clara brought Violet outside to the backyard.

"Whoa," said Violet as she gazed at the woods. "That's a lot of nature."

"I wasn't too thrilled at first," Addie said. "But now we love it."

"And we have cool new neighbor

friends," said Clara, pointing to both sides of their backyard. "Over there is Oliver, and over here is Morgan. She's awesome. She's, like, Addie's new best friend."

"Clara!" scolded Addie. She looked at Violet, and saw the look of deep hurt on Violet's face. "She'll never be my *best* best friend," Addie told her. "That will always be you."

Addie held up the bracelet Sky Dance had made for her with magic and showed Violet the locket with their photo inside.

Violet's eyes teared up. She swallowed hard. "Same here," she said.

Then she sat down on the grass and started crying.

"Oh my gosh," said Addie, kneeling beside her friend. "What's wrong?"

Violet sniffled. "I—I miss you so much,

Addie. What's school going to be like without you there?"

"You have all our other friends," said Addie.

"But they aren't you!" Violet hung her head, then ran her fingers through her hair. "Also, I hate this haircut. It's too short!"

"I like it," said Clara, kneeling on the other side of Violet. "It makes you look more grown-up."

"Really?" sniffled Violet. "I keep thinking it makes me look like I'm five. Because this is the haircut I had when I was five!" She let out a few more sobs. "Although I guess it helps that I have a PIMPLE on my chin! That also helps me look older!"

Violet began to cry again, and Addie let her. She knew from experience that when her friend was sad, it was best to wait a few minutes before trying to cheer her up. Clara caught Addie's glance and started making weird hand gestures. She was pointing to Violet, then pretending she was flapping her wings, then catching an invisible something in her hands.

Addie stood up, grabbed her sister's hand, and pulled her away.

"What on earth are you trying to say?" asked Addie.

"Duh," said Clara in frustration. "Violet is the perfect person to catch and release Spring Shine! Obviously, she needs a wish!"

"Oh my gosh," exclaimed Addie. "You're right!"

"What is she right about?" asked Violet.

Addie paused. Was it safe to tell Violet about the Wishing Wings? She didn't live in Brook Forest, so maybe it would be okay. It would definitely make things easier if Violet knew how to help Spring Shine earn her magic.

Clara gave Addie a nod, and Addie took a deep breath.

"Violet," she began. "We have something incredible to tell you, but you have to promise not to tell anyone else."

"Okay," said Violet, looking curious, but also a little worried.

Addie bit her lip. Where should she even start?

ADDIE!

The sudden voice in Addie's head sounded full of panic.

SOMETHING TERRIBLE HAS HAPPENED!

It was Sky Dance sending a thought

message. Addie saw Clara freeze and knew that she must be hearing from Shimmer Leaf, too.

Spring Shine has disappeared! continued Sky Dance's message. *Madame Furia saw her leaving the grove with a group of purple spiders. Spring Shine told her that the spiders were helping her find the other white butterflies in the woods so she can live with them.*

Madame Furia was a caterpillar who'd been forbidden to turn into a butterfly when she was younger. It was her punishment for becoming jealous of another caterpillar and trying to frame her for a crime she didn't commit. But now Furia was kind and helpful, a good friend to Sky Dance and Shimmer Leaf's mother, Queen Rose Glow.

"This is bad!" said Clara.

"What's bad?" asked a confused Violet.

We're coming to you, came the next message from Sky Dance. *Together we'll figure out what to do next.*

"Looks like we have to find some purple spiders," said Addie to Clara.

"Purple spiders?" asked Violet. "I've never heard of those."

Addie sat back down next to Violet.

"I'll explain everything," Addie told her. "Are you ready for the best secret ever?"

CHAPTER FOUR

M agic," said Violet, her voice flat. "Butterflies," she added, even flatter.

"Yes!" Addie insisted as excitedly as she could. "Magic butterflies!"

"Who grant wishes!" chimed in Clara. "And talk! And are basically awesome!"

Violet gave Addie and Clara a dirty look and drew in a deep, irritated breath.

"I came all the way here to surprise you, and now you guys are messing with me for fun? That is so not okay."

"I would never in a million years mess with you!" cried Addie. "Violet, you have to believe us!"

Addie felt Clara whispering in her ear. "We don't have time to convince her. Sky Dance and Shimmer Leaf will show her the magic when they get here."

"That's true," Addie whispered back. "Okay, let's focus on the purple spiders. I wonder if they come into Brook Forest or only live in the woods?"

"That would be a good first thing to figure out," Clara replied. "Let's find a spider and ask."

Clara walked away and started wandering around the backyard, scanning it for spiderwebs. Addie turned to Violet, who was hugging her legs to her chest, looking confused and annoyed. *Great,* thought Addie, *Violet is going to spend this whole visit mad at me!* How could she make things right?

"Violet," said Addie, standing up and reaching out her hand to her friend. "You don't have to believe us. Hopefully you will soon. In the meantime, can we show you the woods?"

Violet's eyes lit up now. Back in the city, Addie had steered clear of anything having to do with nature, but Violet was the opposite. She loved collecting rocks wherever she went, and digging in the mud after a rainstorm. Magic or no magic, Addie knew Violet would love to do some exploring.

Violet smiled, grabbed Addie's hand, and let Addie pull her up. Together, they walked between two of the trees that bordered the backyard.

"Here's a web!" called Clara, who was standing next to a thorny bush. When the other girls reached her, Clara bent down to the web.

"Hello!" called Clara. "Anyone home?"

Violet rolled her eyes. "If you're going to keep playing the magic-bug game," she said, "I'm going to see what I can find in the dirt over there." Addie watched as Violet picked up a large stick and started poking around the roots of a large oak. *Sky Dance and Shimmer Leaf better get here soon!* she thought.

"Let's look over that way," suggested Clara to Addie, pulling her toward a large, fallen branch lying on the ground. Sure enough, there was a web strung in

the "Y" of the branch. A small brown spider was busy working there. It didn't look at all magical.

"Pardon me," said Clara extra-politely to the spider. "Can I ask you a few questions?"

No answer. The spider kept spinning its web.

"This could take forever," said Addie

with a sigh. But then something caught her eye up ahead. There was an old tree stump that seemed to be twinkling in the sunlight. She drew closer. Clara followed.

It was another web, stretched from the top of the tree stump to a rock on the ground. The strands looked thicker than other webs. When the light hit them, they shone like silver. Addie saw flecks of color in there too.

"Purple!" she burst out. "It's purple!"

"Bingo!" exclaimed Clara, then went back into her polite mode. "Ahem. Madam Spider? Or Mister Spider?"

Suddenly, a deep, rough voice came from inside the stump.

"I prefer *Sir Spider*, thank you very much. Why are you bothering me?"

The sisters exchanged an excited look.

"We need some help, Sir Spider," said Addie, trying to sound as grown-up as possible. "Would you speak with us for a few moments?"

There was a long silence while Addie crossed all her fingers and toes. *Please please please!* she thought. Finally, a tiny purple leg poked out of a crack in the tree stump. Followed by another, and another, and then the rest of the spider. Sir Spider was very big and very, very purple.

He looked at Addie and Clara and said grumpily, "Okay, then. I'm here. What do you want?"

When the light hit the spider's back, it lit up in sparkles. The sparkles didn't match his crankiness at all.

"We're looking for purple spiders who might know something about a Wishing Wing," said Clara.

Sir Spider waved two of his legs dismissively. "Eh, I don't get involved in spider drama. Check with the spider next door." He pointed both legs toward Morgan's backyard.

The girls thanked him and went over to Violet, who was holding an earthworm she'd pulled out of the ground.

"Want to come meet my neighbor?" asked Addie.

Violet looked toward Morgan's yard and a shadow of jealousy crossed her face. "Okay," she said, but didn't sound at all excited about it.

Once they stepped into the yard, they followed voices to Morgan's playhouse. Through the playhouse window, Addie could see Morgan and Oliver. They were sweeping and dusting, getting the playhouse ready to be used again after months of neglect.

"It's so cool that they're friends again!" Addie muttered to Clara, and Clara nodded in agreement. That had been the happiest result of their adventure with Blue Rain.

"Hey, guys!" said Morgan as she and Oliver came out to meet them.

"Morgan, Oliver, this is Violet, our friend from the city," said Addie.

Violet glanced at Addie, looking even more bummed out than before (if that was possible).

"That's all I am now?" asked Violet. "Your *friend from the city?*"

"Violet, no!" said Addie. "You're many things, and all of them are special to me."

Violet half-smiled, with only one

side of her mouth. It was better than nothing.

"We're looking for spiderwebs," said Clara. "Cool-looking ones. Seen any?"

"We just swept up a bunch from the playhouse," replied Morgan. "One was really thick! It was crazy!"

No! thought Addie. *You destroyed a magical web!*

This day was really not going the way it should. Her best friend was getting madder and madder at her. She and Clara were no closer to finding out where Spring Shine had gone. And why hadn't Sky Dance and Shimmer Leaf shown up yet?

Also, there was this super-annoying buzzing around her ear. Addie swatted at what was probably a fly.

Now it was buzzing around her other

ear. She caught sight of a bee and turned her head away.

Wait a sec, she thought. *A BEE!*

She turned back to the bee, just in time to see it land on her shoulder.

"Addie!" said a familiar voice close to her ear. This was no ordinary bee; this was Kirby. He was their friend, and he was great at lending a hand—or a wing, rather—when they needed it most.

"Hi, you!" Addie whispered.

"I thought you should know, I saw a purple spider hanging from a tree over that way, in between Morgan's yard and your yard. She was complaining that she'd just lost her web because two kids destroyed it."

"Will you show me?" asked Addie.

Kirby answered by flying off toward their yard. Addie followed, glancing over her shoulder to see Violet giving her a confused look. She held up her hand to say *I'll be right back!*

Kirby stopped and pointed. High up in a tree, swinging from a glittering silver strand, a purple spider was muttering to itself.

Addie stood underneath it and waved.

"Hi," she said. "I'm Addie. I heard you lost your web."

"Yes!" said the spider, sounding frustrated. "That's the third time this week!"

"I'm so sorry to hear that. This is my yard over here. You're welcome to spin a web anywhere you want. My sister and I will do our best to make sure nobody destroys it."

The spider twirled to examine Addie's yard, then twirled back. "That would be lovely, but why are you being so nice to a spider?"

"I'm hoping you can help me find a Wishing Wing butterfly named Spring Shine."

The spider lowered herself so she was dangling right in front of Addie's face. Her tiny purple eyes stared into Addie's.

"Well," began the spider, "I did have a visit from an Elder Spider earlier. He said he'd been in the woods spinning webs to slow down some humans. I'm guessing you're one of them. He also told me to be on the lookout for a New Bloom with rainbows on her wings."

"That's Spring Shine!" exclaimed Addie. "Have you seen her?"

"No," said the spider, shaking her head. The motion made her swing back and forth on her web strand. "But I heard some other spiders did, and brought her to the Crystal Web."

"What's the Crystal Web?" Addie asked.

"That's where all the Elder Spiders live, in the heart of the woods. Not a place for humans, to be sure."

"You've been so helpful!" said Addie. "Kirby here can help you find a safe spot in my yard. I highly recommend the space under the back deck. My sister and I are the only ones who can fit in there, and we won't disturb your home!"

The spider tilted her head at Addie, probably deciding whether or not to trust her, then nodded and swung to the next tree over. Then to another and another, with Kirby following, until she landed somewhere in the grass and disappeared.

Clara and Violet came running up.

"Why did you wander off?" asked Clara. "Did you find something?"

"I'm going inside!" announced Violet. "If you don't want to spend time with me, I'm going to tell my parents we should leave now."

"Violet, no," Addie begged.

Flit-flit.

Something fluttered past them. Addie saw Clara hold out her hand. Shimmer Leaf!

Addie held out her own hand and in a blink, Sky Dance was landing on her palm. "Hey, stranger!" said the Wishing Wing.

"Sorry it took us so long!" added Shimmer Leaf.

Addie looked at Violet. Violet was staring at the two butterflies, her eyes wide with amazement.

"Violet," laughed Addie, relief and happiness rushing through her. "Meet Sky Dance and Shimmer Leaf. Sky and Shimmer, this is Violet."

"Hi!" said Sky Dance to Violet. "I've heard so much about you!"

Violet closed her eyes tight, shook her head hard, and opened them again.

"This isn't happening," she said.

Then she turned away.

CHAPTER FIVE

Violet!" Addie called, stepping toward her friend. She put her hand on Violet's shoulder and Violet spun back around. She had tears in her eyes.

"This is crazy," said Violet. "You and I always talked about what real magic would be like—and now you've actually found it!"

She believed!

Addie wrapped her friend into a super-tight hug. *Now* it felt like old times.

"Remember the friendship bracelets we made each other before I left?" Addie asked Violet.

Violet broke free of the hug and rolled up her sleeve to show Addie her wrist. There it was: the blue, red, green, and yellow bracelet Addie had made. She'd wanted it to look like a rainbow.

Addie held up her own wrist and said, "Sky Dance turned mine into this, and put some magic in there to keep our connection strong."

Sky Dance flitted off of Addie's shoulder and landed on Violet's.

"Would you like one of your own?" she asked Violet. "Then you two can match!"

"Yes, please!" said Violet.

"Then hold out your arm and watch!"

Sky Dance shot into the air and then swooped down toward Violet's wrist, flying her first circle. She left behind a trail of pink and turquoise as she curled into a second circle, and then a third. The spiral of colors reminded Addie of a fancy lollipop she once saw at a candy store. The look of total wonder on Violet's face made Addie crack up. It took a lot to wow Violet, but this was a no-brainer!

When the colors faded into sparkling bursts of light, then finally disappeared, Addie and Clara moved closer to see the

result. Violet's bracelet was now a gold chain, just like Addie's, with a matching heart locket. Violet opened it. Inside was the same photo of Addie and Violet.

"Oh. My. Gosh," said Violet. She stared at the bracelet for a few more seconds, then looked up with a big grin. "So! We have some purple spiders to find! Let's go, slowpokes!"

Violet marched into the woods. Addie and Clara exchanged a look and started laughing, then ran to catch up with their friend. Sky Dance flitted alongside Addie, and Addie filled her in on what the purple spider had said about the Crystal Web.

"The heart of the woods?" asked Sky Dance.

"That's what she said. I'm guessing

it means the center of the woods? We should find a map."

Sky Dance stopped flying and hovered in the air for a moment, pondering something.

"It *could* mean the center," she said. "But it could also mean the Heart. With a capital H."

"There's a difference?" asked Addie.

"I've never been there, but I once overheard Mama talk about a special cave. The entrance is shaped just like a heart, so it's sometimes called . . ."

"The Heart of the Woods!" Addie exclaimed. "That makes sense. Do you know where to find it?"

"I know it's on the other side of Breezy Pond. I can get us that far, but then we'll have to search from there."

Addie gathered the others and filled them in on their destination.

"A cave." Violet sighed. "This is turning out to be the best day ever."

Sky Dance and Shimmer Leaf led the way toward Breezy Pond, further into the woods than Addie or Clara had been yet. Addie knew the butterflies would never let her get lost, but it still made Addie nervous to be in such unfamiliar territory. There were no friendly baby-elephant rocks here.

Eventually the trees gave way to a clearing, and beyond the clearing's tall grass, Addie could see something blue and rippling. It was a pond, reflecting the clear sky above. The water moved this way and that in the slight wind. Breezy Pond was definitely a good name for it!

The butterfly sisters led the three girls

around the edge of the pond. When they got to the other side, Addie saw Sky Dance land on a tree branch and stretch out her antennae. Everyone was quiet as Sky Dance listened.

"It's this way," she finally said, taking off in a certain direction.

"How do you know?" asked Shimmer Leaf.

"I don't. Not for sure. But Mama keeps telling me to trust my antennae, so that's what I'm doing."

That must be the butterfly version of 'trust your gut,' thought Addie, and smiled.

After a few minutes, they climbed up a hill. As the ground became flat again, there it was: a huge rock cave built into another hill. Its entrance was shaped exactly like a giant heart.

All three girls paused to admire it. "Whoa," said Violet, and Addie felt that summed it up perfectly.

Addie and Violet stepped into the entrance, running their fingers over the rock. It felt smooth and cold and a little wet. Addie had expected it to be dark in the cave, but it wasn't. The space was filled with a soft, warm glow.

Then Addie realized why. Not far from the entrance, an enormous, glassy spiderweb stretched from the roof of the cave to the ground, radiating light. The Crystal Web, which also lived up to its name.

"Addie!" called a tiny, shaky voice.

Addie looked up. Nothing there. She glanced left, then right. Where was the voice coming from?

"Down here!" it squeaked.

Addie followed the noise to a small hole in the cave wall. The opening of the hole was criss-crossed with spiderweb strands. Behind the strands, trapped in the hole, Addie could see a rainbow of colors.

"Spring Shine!" shouted Addie.

The others rushed to see. Sure enough, there was the New Bloom, trapped in a little dungeon.

"We'll take care of these bars," said Clara, reaching out to pull the strands away.

Then a deep voice echoed through the cave.

"INTRUDERS! BE GONE!"

Addie looked up to see three enormous purple spiders hanging on three long, silvery strands from the roof of the cave.

"You tricked Spring Shine!" Addie called to them. "Why are you keeping her prisoner?"

The biggest spider, in the middle, replied, "Only for a short while. We have orders to hold her here until sunset. When her wings turn white, we'll let her go."

"But you know she needs to be caught and released to earn her magic!" Addie put her arm around Violet's shoulder. "We have a human who needs a wish. It'll just take a second!"

"We have our orders!" said the spider on the right.

"Orders?" repeated Addie. "Orders from who? Who's bossing you around?"

The spiders swung on their strands so they were close to each other, and started whispering amongst themselves. One of them—the one on the left—seemed rather upset, growing more and more angry. The other two got angry back. Then they swung apart.

"We can't say," said the spider in the middle.

"So go away," said the spider on the right.

Both spiders looked at the spider on the left, waiting for it to add something. There were several long moments of very thick silence.

The spider on the left took in a deep

breath, then paused. "Mind your own—"
She paused. "No! I can't! I won't! I refuse
to go along with her anymore!"

She started lowering herself to the
ground, and the other spiders did the same
in order to chase her. Addie watched
as she scurried toward the cave wall
where Spring Shine's dungeon had been
spun. She was almost there. Addie's
heart leaped! Once Spring Shine could
fly free, the spiders wouldn't be able to
catch her.

"STOP!" called a voice.

Addie looked up. Another purple spider
was swinging into the cave, but it wasn't
alone. Its legs were wrapped around something. Something bright green, and long,
with touches of red in it.

"Madame Furia!" shouted Clara.

The spider and Madame Furia landed on a rock in front of the girls. The spider's legs were still locked tightly onto the caterpillar. *Poor Madame Furia!* thought Addie. *She'll be lunch!*

"Don't you dare eat her!" warned Addie. "She's our friend!"

The spider froze. Madame Furia's big red eyes fixed on Addie. Addie couldn't read the expression, but figured it must be something along the lines of *Thank you for rescuing me!*

Then Furia turned her head toward the spider. "Thanks for the ride," she said. "Now, be gone."

"Yes, ma'am!" squeaked the spider, who released Furia and scurried away.

Wait, thought Addie. *What exactly is happening?*

Madame Furia faced Addie, Clara, Violet, Sky Dance, and Shimmer Leaf. She looked annoyed, but also amused.

"All right, then," said Furia slowly, "time to deal with all of you!"

CHAPTER SIX

Madame Furia, who had always been sweet and helpful to them, was now smiling a downright evil smile. The red spikes on her back suddenly looked extra-sharp.

"Madame Furia?" asked Addie. "What are you doing here?"

Madame Furia threw her head back

and laughed hard. The laugh traveled down the length of her body, jiggling it segment by segment.

"What am I doing here?" Furia echoed. "Why, my dear! I'm finishing what I began!"

"YOU!" shouted Clara, stepping close and stomping her foot, her hands on her hips. It was what Addie wished she could do, if she weren't frozen in surprise. "*You* cast the curse on the New Blooms!"

"I certainly did," said Furia, puffing up with pride.

A million questions filled Addie's head. The first ones to pop out of her mouth were: "Why? How?"

Madame Furia slowly lifted herself, bit by bit, so she was standing up straight on her hindmost legs. She definitely looked tall, and very creepy, like this. Addie noticed that strapped to one of Furia's legs was a tiny bag made of woven grass.

"Why?" said Furia. "Why do you think? Since I was forbidden to become a Wishing Wing, it was up to me to create my own magic! I designed the enchantment so that every 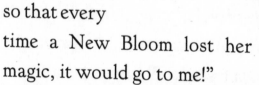 time a New Bloom lost her magic, it would go to me!"

"I don't get it," said Clara. "How did you cast an enchantment if you don't have your own magic?"

Furia looked at Clara with one red eye. Her other eye swiveled toward Addie, then Violet, then toward Spring Shine in her little cell.

"Oh, fine," sighed Furia. "I might as well tell you. It's too late for you to do anything about it. Do you remember my tale about wandering the woods after my punishment in Wishing Wing Grove?"

Addie nodded. She did, for sure. The image of a sad, lonely Madame Furia had stuck in her head ever since the caterpillar had shared her story.

"In my travels," continued Furia, "I came upon an enormous old tree, larger than I'd ever seen. The trunk had tiny holes in it. I crawled through, hoping the trunk was hollow so I could make a little home for myself in there. I was right: it *was* hollow, but it wasn't empty! Inside that tree trunk was a plant I'd never seen before, made completely of gold. I knew it was special, but I was also very hungry. So I ate a leaf, then went to sleep. The next morning, it was raining, and I found myself reciting a little poem we learned in the caterpillar nursery: *Rain, rain, go away, come again some other day.* The second I finished saying that, the rain stopped!"

"The plant gave you magic?" asked Addie.

"Temporary magic, yes. I found out later that it is the Tree of Togetherness, planted ages ago as a gesture of peace by the rulers of the four enchanted realms in these woods: the butterflies, wasps, bees, and spiders. If I eat one leaf, it gives me the ability to cast one spell."

"So you cast a spell on the New Blooms!" said Clara.

"It was a brilliant one, too. Planned so that it worked differently with each butterfly. My only mistake was not guessing that Queen Rose Glow would send for human help. You girls have kept me from stealing the magic of the first three New Blooms, but this last one is mine!"

One of the Elder Spiders—the one in the middle—swung low toward Madame Furia.

"You used Tree of Togetherness magic to make us follow your orders?" he asked.

"Yes, yes," sighed Furia. "The spiders, the bees, and the wasps. One spell each. It was so easy!"

"My fellow elders!" cried the spider. "Let's grab her!"

The other two spiders swung toward

Furia. As they did, Furia raised herself up even higher on her back legs and shouted a spell.

"Purple spiders, now you dangle, but not for long; let's watch you tangle!"

Furia knocked her two front legs together, and a golden lightning bolt shot out of them. The spiders' web strands bumped against one another and twisted together, and the three spiders began to spin toward the Crystal Web. The web caught them and wrapped them all up in a little ball.

Furia laughed. "Good thing I ate a golden leaf right before I came here. Let's see how long it takes them to get out of that one!"

Addie turned to Clara and Violet, and pointed toward Furia. They knew what she was trying to say. *Let's catch her!*

Violet was the one who stepped toward Furia first. She reached out both hands and started to scoop up the caterpillar.

"Ow!" shrieked Violet, dropping Furia to the ground. Violet started rubbing her hands together, fighting back tears.

Furia laughed. "That was the spell I came up with this morning! It made my spikes so sharp that anyone or anything that touches me would get jabbed."

Addie put her arm around Violet and rubbed her friend's hand. "That must have hurt!"

Out of the corner of her eye, Addie saw Sky Dance and Shimmer Leaf exchange a knowing glance.

There's only one way to work against magic like that, Sky Dance now told Addie in a thought message. *More magic!*

Addie leaned in toward Violet's ear. "Watch this," she whispered.

Sky Dance and Shimmer Leaf flew up toward the roof of the cave, then in a big circle along the cave walls. Addie was confused at first, but then realized they needed room to pick up some speed. They rushed toward Madame Furia so quickly that Furia didn't have time to react. The two butterflies touched wings and flew a circle around the caterpillar. The ribbon of light they left behind was pink, turquoise, purple, peach, and mint green, and sparkled brighter than ever.

They flew behind Addie, Clara, and Violet, then back around Madame Furia.

"Oh no, you don't!" shouted Furia. She opened the woven grass bag she was carrying and pulled out a golden leaf.

But the cloud of glittering colors settled over the caterpillar like a fog, carrying the leaf out of Furia's grip and into the swirling air. Sky Dance and Shimmer Leaf picked up even more speed and flew another circle, and then finally a third.

It was hard for Addie to see the butterflies now, because suddenly there were fireworks in her eyes. She had to close them for a moment. When Addie opened them, she realized everything looked much bigger.

That meant she was much smaller! *Butterfly-size!*

Addie stretched out one arm and sure enough, it wasn't an arm. It was a wing, magenta and powder blue with a lavender heart pattern. Whenever Wishing

Wing magic turned her into a butterfly, she came out looking like this.

She looked for Clara and Violet, but they weren't there. Instead, there were two other butterflies.

Addie recognized one: its wings were the deep pink and orange of a sunset, patterned with flames. That was Clara!

But who was the other butterfly? The one with purple flowers on her yellow-and-green wings?

Oh, duh!

"Violet!" cried Addie.

"What on earth just happened?" asked Clara.

Violet's butterfly eyes stared at Addie, then at Clara, then glanced around her. She jumped when she glimpsed one of her own wings.

"Am I . . ." Violet started to say, but was too shocked to finish.

"A butterfly! Yes!" replied Addie. "I'm not sure how it happened, but cool!"

Sky Dance and Shimmer Leaf fluttered past in another circle. The trail they left behind was fading, the colors not as strong.

Without really thinking about it, Addie called out to Clara and Violet. "Let's fly with Sky Dance and Shimmer Leaf!"

Addie knew she and the other girls didn't have magic like the Wishing Wings, but at least the butterfly sisters would know they weren't alone in their battle against Madame Furia.

Addie lifted herself into the air, and Clara did too.

"How do I do that?" called Violet.

"Just imagine flying!" Addie replied.

"It's like running, but in the air!" added Clara.

Addie didn't think her friend would have trouble with flying . . . and she was right. It only took a couple of experimental wing-flaps before Violet was off the ground.

"Oh. My. Gosh!" she squealed.

"Come on," laughed Addie. "We'll show our friends that we have their backs!"

CHAPTER SEVEN

W hat in the woods?" exclaimed Shimmer Leaf when she saw that Addie, Clara, and Violet were now butterflies, zooming through the cave.

"I have no idea how it happened!" Addie shouted as she fluttered alongside Sky Dance. "But we're here, and we're with you."

Clara flew next to Shimmer Leaf.

Violet was a little slow at first, but soon she was keeping up with them on the other side of Sky Dance.

The five butterflies started another circle around Madame Furia, who pulled out another leaf and began gobbling it up. Addie glanced over her shoulder and couldn't believe what she saw.

The trail of colors had changed. It wasn't just Sky Dance's and Shimmer Leaf's colors, like before. Now the rainbow was wider, striped with magenta, powder blue, and lavender—Addie's colors—along with pink and orange, which were Clara's colors! She also saw the violet, green, and yellow of Violet's wings.

After they finished their loop around Furia, the colors swirled together into a thick, glittering cloud that settled over the caterpillar. Addie flew close enough to hear Furia try one last spell, glaring at them. It was the most frustrated, angry look Addie had ever seen on anyone—human or insect.

"Fly no more, you meddling girls!" shouted Furia. *"I turn your antennae back into curls!"*

She knocked her front legs together, and a golden lightning bolt shot out. But this time, the bolt vanished as soon as it hit the cloud.

"No!" Furia cried. She shuddered, lowering her body down segment by segment.

The many colors of the cloud turned into sparkles that landed on Furia like snowflakes. Sky Dance, Shimmer Leaf, and all three butterfly-girls flitted toward the ground. It felt extra-hard and solid on Addie's six little feet.

She watched as the sparkles themselves faded. When she could see Madame Furia again, she was curled up into a ball as if trying to hide inside herself.

The fireworks flashed in Addie's eyes, and she knew what that meant. Back to being human! Before she knew it, she had transformed again. She turned and saw Clara and Violet's magic wearing off.

Clara examined her own hands, as if making sure she still had the same ones and the right number of fingers. "I don't understand," she said. "How did Sky Dance and Shimmer Leaf turn us all into butterflies? I thought they needed the Queen and King's help to do that!"

"As did I," said a voice above them. Addie glanced up to see Rose Glow and Flit Flash glide to a landing between the girls and Madame Furia. Rose Glow looked long and hard at Addie and Clara, tilting her furry red head one way, then another.

"Here's what I believe happened," continued the Queen. "Furia had a golden leaf that got mixed in with Sky Dance's and Shimmer Leaf's magic, giving it extra power to change you three girls. Then, your show of support for your friends made everything stronger still. Strong enough to destroy Furia's anger and jealousy."

"That makes sense!" said Sky Dance.

"I'm glad the leaf was used for something good rather than wicked," added Shimmer Leaf.

They all turned to Madame Furia.

She had uncurled herself, but was now

hanging her head, her eyes drooping low. Big green tears fell from them onto the floor of the cave.

Addie opened her mouth to say something, but stopped. Maybe this was another of Furia's tricks. After all, she *had* fooled everyone into thinking she was a kind and harmless caterpillar.

Then Furia whispered something. Addie leaned in.

"I'm . . ." Furia began, then sobbed. "I'm . . . so . . . sorry."

Now everyone gathered close to hear what she had to say.

"I never meant for it to go this far," continued Furia. "But when I saw those four New Blooms in their chrysalides,

waiting to burst out as beautiful butterflies, I felt so very jealous! That's always
been my problem. I just couldn't control
myself this time."

"I know all about jealousy," said Clara.
"I have a big sister . . ."

Furia gave a sad little smile at that.

"I'm deeply, deeply sorry," said Furia. "I
know you'll never forget what I've done,
but I hope you can forgive me. That's all I
ask. Then I'll be on my way." She inched
slowly toward Rose Glow. "Thank you
for all your kindness, my dear old friend.
I regret that I took advantage of it."

Furia moved slowly past the Queen
and King on her way out of the cave.
Addie had never seen anything as sor-
rowful or lonely in her life . . . and hoped
she never would again.

Rose Glow whispered something into

Flit Flash's antennae. He tilted his head, then nodded.

"Golden Burst, wait!" she called to Madame Furia.

The caterpillar froze, then slowly turned. "You called me by my caterpillar name . . ." murmured Furia.

"That's who you will always be to me," Rose Glow said warmly. "And I believe that's who you still are, in your heart. Except maybe now you've learned a long overdue lesson about jealousy."

"Are you saying . . ."

"Yes, Golden Burst. I forgive you!"

Furia puffed up and turned a brighter shade of green. "Oh, dear Queen! Thank you!"

Rose Glow smiled and sighed. "I think the outside you should reflect the inside you," she added. "I think you should become the butterfly you've always longed to be."

"Are you sure?" asked the caterpillar hopefully.

"Absolutely sure. But first, Spring Shine must earn her magic. Agreed?"

"Yes, yes! Of course!"

Addie turned to Violet and poked her in the ribs. "That means you! You're up!" She pointed toward Spring Shine's cell, where Spring Shine was watching with her face pressed against the web strands. Violet scrambled to standing, reached over to the strands, and pulled them apart. They came away in her fingers like holiday tinsel.

Spring Shine whooshed gleefully into the air. Violet held out her hands, cupping her palms so they made a perfect nest for the butterfly. When Spring Shine landed there, Violet put one palm over the other and giggled.

"I can feel her wings tickling my hands," said Violet. "Can I let her go now?"

Rose Glow nodded. Violet opened her hands and Spring Shine flew straight up, letting out a "Yippee!" as she flew over to the entrance of the cave. She landed on the edge of the puddle they had stepped over earlier, and peered at her reflection in the water.

Addie held her breath. Was the curse broken? Would Spring Shine be able to see how beautiful she really was?

"Wow!" said Spring Shine. "Not bad!"

"You can see your wing patterns now?" asked Violet.

"Yes! I was so silly for not believing you!"

Spring Shine flew a wide, joyful figure

eight above everyone, then landed on Violet's shoulder.

"So now it's wish time!" she told Violet. "Have you thought about what to ask for?"

Addie watched Violet's face as it got very serious. She looked at Addie and said, "This is really hard."

"I know," replied Addie. "Been there. But don't think about *things* or *stuff*. Think about what will truly make you happy, deep inside."

Violet nodded and closed her eyes. After several long moments, she opened them again.

"Okay. I've got it," said Violet. She took a deep breath. "You know what I wish the most? I wish I had more confidence in myself."

Spring Shine stared at Violet, her

bead-like eyes wide and thoughtful. "That is a great wish," she said. "I can relate."

Violet laughed. "Thanks."

"Go scoop some of that puddle water into your hands," said Spring Shine.

Violet frowned at Addie, and Addie gave her a quick nod. It said, *these Wishing Wings know what they're doing*. Violet bent down with her hands in the bowl-shape again, and scooped up as much puddle water as she could. She showed it to Spring Shine.

"Now what?"

"Hold still," said Spring Shine. She flew one, two, then three circles around Violet's hands, trailing a beautiful rainbow behind her. When the sparkling bursts of color faded, Addie looked to see what the magic had left behind.

A mirror.

Violet held it up and turned it around. The non-mirror side was covered in glittering rainbow stripes.

"It's, uh, very pretty," said Violet.

"This isn't just any mirror," said Spring Shine, landing on Violet's shoulder. "It's got magic in it. When you look at your reflection in that glass, you'll always see how kind and strong you are. If you're ever feeling down about yourself, check the mirror."

Violet held up the mirror again and gazed into it. Her eyes lit up and a big smile spread across her face.

"Thank you!" said Violet, with more happiness than Addie had seen in her friend in a long time.

"I can feel the Wishing Wing magic at its full strength now," said Rose Glow. "It'll be more than enough for what comes next."

Rose Glow rocketed up and fluttered a circle around Furia. Then a second, and a third. Her trail of red, green, and silver seemed brighter than before. Addie could tell Rose Glow was using the most powerful magic she had. The colors and sparkles danced in the air for a long time, but when they finally dissolved, the caterpillar was gone!

In its place was a dazzling butterfly, bright yellow with pink and purple star patterns on its wings.

Rose Glow landed next to the butterfly and smiled affectionately. "Welcome, Golden Burst. It feels wonderful to call you that again."

Golden Burst bowed her head to the Queen, then shook out her new wings. Slowly, she began to flap them. *How strange and amazing it must feel,* thought Addie, *to want wings so badly for so long, and finally get them.*

Within seconds, the new butterfly was in the air. Flying. And laughing. And then, singing!

"Do you really think she'll be okay with never having magic?" Sky Dance asked Rose Glow.

"There are many different types of magic," replied Rose Glow. "Sometimes you are gifted with it, and sometimes you have to make your own, with your decisions and actions." She glanced at Addie, Clara, and Violet. "Golden Burst will find a way to do that, I'm sure."

❧ ❧ ❧

Three girls and three butterflies crossed the line of trees that separated the woods from Addie's backyard.

Addie knew she should feel happy. They had broken the enchantment and saved all four New Blooms! Plus, she was so proud of how brave she'd been in the last few days. But underneath those feelings was a bittersweet sadness. Their adventure was over. They would no longer see Sky Dance, Shimmer Leaf, and their other magical friends every day. Plus, Violet would be leaving to go home soon. What would happen now?

Sky Dance landed on her shoulder. She must have sensed Addie's thoughts.

"It'll be okay, said the butterfly. "I'll visit you, and you'll visit me."

"Same here," added Violet, stepping up onto Addie's other side and taking her hand.

Addie laughed. How could she feel sad when she was surrounded by such great friends?

Suddenly, Addie heard her mother's voice calling. "Hey, girls? We're going to have a barbecue and could use your help!"

"We'll be right there!" Addie called back.

"We should flutter along," said Sky Dance, crawling down Addie's arm and into her hand. Addie pulled her close and let Sky Dance's wings tickle her cheek in a butterfly kiss. "But I promise," Sky Dance added, "this is not goodbye. Just 'see you later'."

Violet held out her palm and Spring Shine landed on it. "In our case, much later," Violet said sadly.

Addie knew that Sky Dance had to cast Forgetting Magic on Violet. She wouldn't remember the Wishing Wings, but would still feel her butterfly connection to Spring Shine.

Clara had Shimmer Leaf cupped in her palms, and they were whispering to each other.

"Ready?" Addie asked Sky Dance. Sky Dance nodded. "You guys ready, too?" Addie asked Clara and Violet. They nodded as well.

Addie took a deep breath, then shouted, "One . . . two . . . three!"

Together, the girls opened their palms. The three butterflies sailed into the air, zigzagging playfully around one another as they traveled toward the woods. Addie, Clara, and Violet watched until their flying friends became tiny dots of color . . . and then disappeared in the distance.

Clara and Violet put their arms around Addie in a three-person hug. Addie felt the weight of all her worries about school, and her new life, melt away.

Finally, Clara stepped out of the hug and said, "I know you're all awesome and fearless now, but are you prepared to face Dad's first attempt at a barbecued dinner?"

Addie laughed. "Bring it on!" she said.

A barbecue. A new school. Magic butterflies who may need more help in the future.

Bring them all on!

Read all the books in the
Butterfly Wishes
series!

Jennifer Castle is the author of the Butterfly Wishes series and many other books for children and teens, including *Famous Friends* and *Together at Midnight*. She lives in New York's Hudson Valley with her husband, two daughters, and two striped cats, at the edge of a deep wood that is most definitely filled with magic— she just hasn't found it yet.

www.jennifercastle.com

Tracy Bishop is the illustrator of the Butterfly Wishes series. She has loved drawing magical creatures like fairies, unicorns, and dragons since she was little and is thrilled to get to draw magical butterflies. She lives in the San Francisco Bay Area with her husband, son, and a hairy dog named Harry.

www.tracybishop.com